Some Day My Prince Won't Come

"It can all be changed once people realize that it can be . . ."

For girls like Nicki, Livy, Cath, Shirley and Daisy in these seven short stories, growing up female in today's world presents problems and contradictions as well as challenges and new possibilities.

Rosemary Stones (Ed)

Some Day My Prince Won't Come

More Stories for Young Feminists

LIONS · TRACKS

First published in Great Britain 1988 by Piccadilly Press
Published in Lions Tracks 1990

Lions Tracks is an imprint of
the Children's Division, part of
the Collins Publishing Group
8 Grafton Street, London W1X 3LA

Printed in Great Britain
by William Collins Sons & Co. Ltd, Glasgow

Contents

Stilettos

I'd seen the notice for Saturday work in Ridley's window and rung up. When I got there, the manageress was by the till talking to some other girl. She was being interviewed for the same job before me and she would have got it only the manageress decided that I was better looking. Turns out the manageress's name is Lynette and she's a right bitch.

I don't mean I'm not glad she thought I was nice looking. I know I'm not bad if I'm being honest, although you can't say it about yourself. I've got blue eyes and long brown hair and I don't get spots. My tits are a bit small for my liking (can't think why, my mum and my nan have got enormous ones and I thought it was supposed to run in families) and my bum is a bit big. But the point is I don't think people should get jobs because of what they look like. I felt bad when Lynette said she chose me because nice looking girls are what the customers like. It's only a shoe shop after all.

Lynette's nice looking of course – very black clear skin, small and sort of delicate but with a good figure. She only takes size three shoes.

She doesn't behave like a manageress. She's twenty-four, right, and she gets to say what happens in her shop even if she does have to check with Head Office. I think that's really good. But you should see her with blokes. When there's a half-way decent man about, she starts flirting and simpering and making really crude jokes. She'll even do it with the policemen from Endell Station when they walk past. And what she wears underneath!

Once when the shop was quiet, she left Zoë in charge and me and her went to TopStyle round the corner because she'd heard they'd got some new things in. You should have seen Lynette in the changing room. I wear bikini briefs but if you blinked you'd miss hers. They were just a tiny triangle at the front and a bit of string holding it on. I've seen them kind on sale in shops but I never thought anyone wore them. You could see all her bum. I didn't know where to look but Lynette's going: "Here Nicki, try this on! How d'you think I look in this?" so I suppose that's what she wears every day. It can't be exactly comfortable, but then again I suppose it turns her boyfriend on. Any money they have a whale of a time when they get home.

Lynette turns out to be a moody cow and all. When she gets the hump, the rest of us can't do nothing right. Even when there's no customers she's screaming at us to stop chatting and get on.

Get on with what? Once she has me lugging a whole consignment of men's shoes up two flights to the stockroom on my own because she has it in for me that day. I was knackered afterwards. I don't think that kind of thing's funny although she obviously did: "Cheer up then, Nicki! There's another twenty cartons coming in next Saturday."

The thing that got me most though was the way she took the piss when me and the other girls talked about anything other than clothes and men: "Setting the world to rights again, girls! Right little brain boxes, you lot, but you don't know nothing about life."

Our shop's just off Mere Street market and there's always some group or other at the end of the market selling their newspapers or handing out leaflets. Sometimes they'll have a placard. It's these two women in Doc Martens quite often selling *Militant* and sometimes this black couple from Anti-Apartheid, with their kids, telling you not to buy things from South Africa. I go along with them. I never buy Outspan oranges and grapes. It's hard though down the market because a lot of the stuff's not labelled and they thing you're mad when you ask where it's from. Sometimes it's the National Front. They look like normal blokes. They don't so much say things to black people going past as look them over and crowd them off the pavement. I've even seen them do it to a black woman on her own with a pushchair and small kids.

One Saturday they're standing there at the usual spot at the end of the market which is almost outside our shop when Lynette sees these two policemen walking by and decides to have a laugh. "Officer!" she goes in some right loud voice, "could you move these people away from my shop. I don't want odd shoes at the end of the day."

"Ain't us that's the thieves round here, love," goes one of them. The police make them move to the opposite corner where we can't see them from the shop. Lynette thinks it's really funny but the fact is she's chancing it. People like that, they can always come back and get you some other time when there won't be two policemen around.

She is good at her job though. She's got a nose for dodgy credit cards. Sometimes it's obvious like when this man had a card with the name Hilary Pulford on it. We all just laughed at him. Afterwards someone told me that you can have men called Hilary – not a Mere Street market roughneck though, somehow. Another time this girl had glued a strip of paper over the name on the card. You can tell by the way they do the signature as well. If they take ages and they're thinking about it, it's stolen. Half of them have a cheque already signed. Lynette takes the card into the back to ring up and most of them leave when she does that. One girl begged and begged to have the card back. She was really pale and ill-looking. Most likely a druggie, Lynette said. Lynette always said if there was real trouble, they could have it – shoes, cards, money. "I'm not getting hurt for the sake of Mr Ridley and his shoes. He won't thank me." Not that she exactly stuck to that when we did have trouble.

It was coming up to my GCSEs. My mum made me promise not to work the weekends before the exams but Lynette phones up to say that Zoë's off sick and can I come to help out. My mum couldn't very well say no to her when Lynette had let her have a staff discount on shoes for herself and for my dad. She's the sort who reminds you.

It's one of those frantic Saturdays and I must have run up to that stockroom about one hundred and fifty times. Lots of stupid people who didn't know their own shoe size and all. Kensington branch rings up to ask if we've got any *Nina* size five left, but I'm so rushed off my feet I just say no without even looking. They sound like a right load of Sloanes, the girls from that Ridley's branch.

I sometimes go into other branches of Ridley's out of curiosity. It's funny to see it all from the outside as a customer.

Anyway, at closing time, Lee (she's the other

Saturday girl) and me are doing the shutters and locking up the front while Lynette's cashing up in the back. Then we hear a kind of scuffling noise. We go in and Lynette's standing there, very quiet for her, with two white blokes, one young looking and skinny with a leather jacket and one older and fat. Then I see the fat one's holding a bit of lead pipe. Lee starts up: "Excuse me, we're closed!" before she sees what's what and shuts up. Then we all just stand there.

"We'll have the key to the safe and a few pairs of shoes and all while we're here, darlings," goes the fat one with the lead pipe in his hand. "You two little tarts can get the shoes sorted while this one," he's looking at Lynette, "can find us that key."

I'm watching Lynette while he's talking. Her eyes are signalling. That's what makes me pull myself together and start thinking – the fact that Lynette's the one most likely to get hurt, yet she's signalling to me and Lee to stay cool. Lee and me don't say nothing. We start piling boxes of shoes into dustbin liner bags. Then the skinny one goes: "Not very sexy these shoes, girls! Ain't you got nothing but old granny shoes?"

"There's this one," says Lee. She's really shaking but she won't let him see it. She gets a pair of *Satin*.

Personally I think *Satin* is a nasty shoe. It's a black satin stiletto with a six inch heel like a dagger and at the back a criss-cross diamante trim over a red satin finish. You know what I mean; right hooker shoes and expensive too.

"Oh, very kinky," goes the fat one, "I'll have a pair of them for the wife and all. Make sure you put in a size five, darling." I'm getting a pair of *Satin* and so's Lee when we catch Lynette's eye again and she nods to us ever so slightly. Then we get it – the heel on *Satin*'s perfect for doing someone an injury.

Just like that Lee smashes the skinny one right on the nose with the point of the *Satin* stiletto heel. At the same time I go for the one with the lead pipe and while I'm hitting him with my *Satin* stiletto, Lynette's twisting his wrist and making him drop the bit of pipe. Then the three of us are out the side door and into the market before the two blokes got time to realize what's hit them.

There's Lynette screaming at the fruit stall men who are packing up their stand for the day, to come and save us. The fruit stall and flower stall blokes go into the side door of the shop like the mob and drag the two thieves out. The little one's nose is bleeding from where Lee hit him.

In the evening paper it's written up as brave-market-traders-rescue-shoe-shop-girls-from-vicious-thugs. Lee and me was really angry but Lynette thinks it's funny. "Don't matter, girls," she goes, "we've got to let them look good

13

sometimes. Most blokes can only just tie their own shoe laces. You two going to start sorting them cartons or not?"

She's all right really, even if she does get on your nerves and everything.

A Family Likeness

"Livy, do you think you'll feel like coming out on Friday?" asked Melanie hesitantly. She'd been building up to asking for at least ten minutes, though she didn't know why she couldn't even ask a simple question any more. Olivia didn't answer; she merely shook her head without bothering to look up. They continued to walk along the road in uneasy silence.

Melanie was getting tired of trying to get things back to normal. Patience didn't come naturally to her and she couldn't get used to having to think about every word and action in case Livy was upset by what she said or did. Yet she felt she had to try, because after all, they were best friends, and best friends stood by each other for better or for worse ... Olivia's whole attitude said very clearly, leave me alone, just let me get on with it, and Melanie was often tempted to do just that. And the worst thing was, she was almost relieved that Livy wanted to be by herself so much, despite the efforts she was making to get her out. She wasn't exactly easy to get on with any more, and she looked so miserable that everybody round her felt miserable too – either that, or guilty because they *weren't* miserable. Sometimes Melanie wondered what it must feel like to have a parent just die on you as Olivia's father had died on her. But the subject was too big and too awful to be contemplated for any length, and Melanie could only push it to the back of her mind as one of those imponderables, like being put in prison for something you didn't do, or living through a nuclear war.

"I wish you would start coming out again," said Melanie, feeling the need to give it one last try. "There isn't any point in moping, he wouldn't have wanted you to . . ." Melanie faltered here; why did she have to mention Livy's father? She might cry or something, which would be awful. But Olivia's face didn't change, she just continued to plod homewards in the mechanical, uninterested way she'd adopted since the funeral last term . . . Melanie suddenly realized it had all been going on for at least three months. How long did the being miserable last? Maybe you never got over it.

Melanie became aware that Livy hadn't even attempted to respond to her question. "Aren't you going to say anything then?" she said crossly, though she wanted to be kind.

"Sorry," said Olivia. "I just don't want to come, that's all."

"OK, fair enough," said Melanie, but she tried to say it gently.

16

They fell into silence again. There was a limit to Melanie's ability to converse with someone who didn't want to talk back – or *couldn't* talk back perhaps. Vaguely, Melanie sensed there were things that Livy wanted to tell her but couldn't put into words. She'd been so silent since it happened, a silence that at times conveyed an angry hostility but at others held nothing but sadness. Melanie was barely able to deal with either. At fifteen, she was beginning to see just how complicated life could be and the idea of spending the next sixty or seventy years in a state of bewilderment was a daunting prospect. She hoped that age would bring wisdom but she had her doubts. Her mother, father and elder sister weren't showing much. Of course, she might manage to be different – wiser, more sensitive and more aware, but if her progress with Livy was anything to go by, she was doomed to a life of ignorance. If only Livy would let her do something, instead of shutting her out all the time . . .

They turned off the High Street and walked towards Olivia's gate. Livy began to fumble in her pocket for her keys. "Do you want to come in?" she said.

Melanie looked at her in surprise. Of late, Livy hadn't seemed able to wait to put the front door between them. "Yes, all right," she said, not really relishing the prospect. Her mother had said that Mrs Everson's grief was such that she was cracking up under the strain. Melanie had never seen anyone cracking up and she wasn't sure she wanted to.

"You don't have to come," said Livy, clearly sensing her reticence.

"No, I'd like to, thanks."

The house hadn't changed, that was something. It was full of nice things, books, plants, pottery and pictures – sketches mostly, done by Livy's dad. She wondered if it hurt Livy to see them on the walls. It would have hurt her had she been in Livy's shoes . . .

Perhaps that was the trouble – up until then their lives had been similar; so similar that they'd been drawn to one another since their first day at school. They'd spotted each other across the playground at the age of just five because they looked so much the same; each had short curly hair and golden coloured skin and later they'd discovered they each had one black parent and one white, that they lived two streets apart and that they both had a birthday in the last week of August. They'd always felt like twins – until last term, that is. Melanie was beginning to realize that if Livy's father could die, then hers could too, that nothing was safe or certain. That was why she didn't want to be in Livy's house and why she felt afraid . . . Why had it been Livy's father and not hers? It could so easily have been her own father who'd died in that accident. Who or what decided things like that? Did it make it better or worse to believe in God?

"Would you like something to drink?" said Livy. "There's cola in the fridge."

"They put teeth in a glass of that stuff and they just disintegrated."

"Does than mean no?"

Melanie smiled. "I guess it does. Have you got any fruit juice?"

"Orange or grapefruit?"

"Orange please."

They sat and looked at each other across the kitchen table, aware that just now, in choosing drinks, they'd almost had a normal conversation.

"Where's your mother?" asked Melanie.

"She'll be back later. She said she'd get some shopping."

"Is she OK?"

"Why shouldn't she be?"

Melanie shrugged. They both knew the answer to that, but perhaps it was better to avoid it.

"Would you like a sandwich?" said Olivia.

Melanie wasn't hungry but Livy had lost so much weight that you could get two people into her jeans. Maybe if she agreed to have a sandwich, Livy would have one too. "What have you got?"

"Ham, cheese, banana, liver pâté . . .'

"Cheese. I'm thinking of becoming a vegetarian."

"Are you?" said Livy. "I tried it once but I only managed to keep it up for a few days. Mum got sick of cooking three separate meals, one for her, one for me and one for dad . . . Cheddar or Edam?" she said briskly, drawing the subject away from her father as if she'd moved there inadvertently and had been stung by the memory.

"Edam," said Melanie, "it's less fattening. I've decided I'm going to have a healthy body – do you know how many people die of heart disease each year?" She stopped abruptly. How crass could you get? She just had to talk about dying. It was rather like needing to laugh in church; the more you didn't want to do something like that, the more you just had to do it. She'd be discussing the cost of funerals next.

Livy began to butter some bread. Melanie noted with satisfaction that she was doing two lots. She looked around the kitchen and her eyes rested on the wall opposite. There was a portrait of Livy's father there – a self-portrait, she supposed. Some time before his death, he'd been hailed as the most outstanding black painter and sculptor of his generation. There was a book about him and he'd been on television.

"Mum put that painting up," said Livy. "I know she thinks of him a lot but she won't talk about him. I wish she would."

20

"It's a nice picture," said Melanie. It was an inadequate thing to say but she couldn't think of anything more. She focused her attention on her sandwich, chewing steadily. Livy had finished hers.

"Would you like to see the others – the other paintings?"

No I wouldn't like, thought Melanie almost fiercely, but she sensed that an honour was being bestowed on her and that it was important to Livy. It was also the first gesture of friendship to come for some time, so she grasped it quickly. "Yes, all right," she said.

The studio was at the top of the house. They went upstairs slowly. "I haven't been in here since he died," said Livy, and Melanie couldn't think of an answer.

The room was light and airy – a window spanned one wall. All around were the trappings of an artist: easels, paints, brushes. There was a black plastic bin full of hardening clay and a powdery dust on the plain wooden floor. As they walked, their footsteps were imprinted on it. Some of the paintings were six feet high. Melanie felt awed by their stature and vibrance. And everywhere, black figures surrounded them, with elongated necks and large heads – heads large enough to house the spirit; Melanie remembered the description from the programme.

Olivia wandered around, and Melanie watched

her with anxiety; what loss was she feeling now? Yet she seemed more relaxed than she'd been for some time; the room seemed to hold something that eased the pain.

"How do you see yourself?" Olivia asked suddenly.

"How do you mean?"

"Do you see yourself as black or white?"

"I don't know. Neither, I suppose. No, *black*."

Olivia nodded. "Me too. That's why what he did was so important."

Melanie knew what she meant. Part of her own sense of herself was somewhere in these paintings and sculptures. How much more was it there for his daughter?

"I wish I was like him," said Livy.

"You are like him. Everybody says so."

"Not just to look at. I want to do what he did."

"Paint?"

"Paint and sculpt."

"Why shouldn't you? You're the best in the school at art – even better than the sixth form."

"Did you know that his father – my grandfather – was a carver too? And his father before him, and back as far as you can imagine?"

Melanie nodded.

"Then it's up to me to carry on or the whole thing will be broken."

"Then carry on," said Melanie quietly.

"I'm not his son."

"What does that matter? You're his daughter."

Olivia was crying; Melanie was trying not to look but she could see it through the corner of her eye. "You're his daughter, Liv, that counts."

"It's always sons."

"He didn't have any sons. Besides, even if he had had them, it would still have been you because you've got the talent – anyone who's seen your paintings would know that."

"But you see, Melanie, I want to do it in order to be part of a tradition, but as a daughter, I can't be part of it, I can only break with it."

Melanie felt out of her depth. She sat on a chair without a back by the window. It was covered with spots of dried paint; it looked like a palette. "Did he say you couldn't do it?"

"No. We didn't discuss it. You see, I couldn't ask him to teach me in case he said no, and he never suggested it. I watched him though, and tried to learn that way. He liked me to be here."

"Perhaps he was waiting until you were old enough to be shown properly."

"I wish I knew. I'm not sure whether he would have shown me or not. I want to do it though."

"Then do it, Livy. Go to art school – do whatever you have to do."

"It won't be the way it should be."

"Nothing ever is. Look, things have changed. Even traditions change – they adapt to suit the times. For your father's father, and all those fathers before him, daughters were for cooking and cleaning, just as for the white slave owners, blacks were for picking cotton and harvesting bananas or whatever it was. It can all be changed once people realize that it can be . . . Oh hell, I don't know how to put this, I can't think how to get it across. But I know I'm right. Your father would want you to be a carver and a painter – he'd probably expect it of you. He wouldn't think you were less able or less important just because you're a daughter rather than a son. Livy, just look at his work. It goes beyond men and women; it even goes beyond black and white."

Olivia looked again. As a small child, she'd watched her father chipping and smoothing rough edges, making something live through the large, shapeless slabs. Figures had appeared as if by magic: men and women and children with long necks and large oval heads, masks with angry, scary faces, horses and strange birds from ancient African mythologies. She'd wanted to emulate him, to carve and paint as he did. Her father had shown her each of the figures he'd created, and told her all the stories. She knew about Anansi and Nyankapon, the First Picni and Brer Rabbit. Since his death, she'd gone over all the legends in her mind, preserving them as the only link she now possessed with her past –

her history. She had been born of a Jamaican father and an English mother, she was British but she was also black, and she'd been afraid that an important part of that identity had been buried with her father. Now she was coming to realize that it could never be lost, just as the spirit of her father could never be lost either; it lived on in the work he'd left behind him and it lived on in her.

Olivia walked round, remembering all her father had taught her, how each piece of wood, each stone held an image waiting to be freed; how the carver simply let it out. She touched each one of the shapes she saw, felt its roughness or its smoothness in her fingertips. She too could free the animals and birds and children trapped in their inanimate materials. And all around the walls, figures looked down at her in paint, in wood, in stone; timeless forms, the spirits of her past brought to life. She saw and felt their colours and was soothed.

She was her father's daughter; she had the right to inherit his skills.

Different Rules

"It's a bit of a mess in here," he said.

"Don't worry about it," I said.

"Not *worried*," he said, "just saying."

He unlocked the door, put his hand inside and switched the light on. I followed him into the room.

"This isn't a *mess*," I said, "more like a war zone."

"Well, I reckon it's *friendly*," he said, "it's got character. D'you want tea or coffee or something?"

"What 'something' have you got?" I said.

"Well," he said, "I've got tea, coffee, tea or coffee."

"In that case I'll have tea."

I unzipped my coat and took it off, threw it over the chair, on top of his jacket.

It's funny when you see somebody else's place for the first time, it's never how you imagined it. There were empty bottles and cans, part of a push-bike, heaps of clothes.

We squeezed past the sofa – a huge blue nylony thing that you had to fight with to get to the kitchen. When I say *kitchen*, I mean a sink, two cupboards and a table, abandoned in one corner.

"What d'you think of the colour scheme then?" he said.

"Um . . . it's not exactly subtle," I said, "sort of . . ."

"Jumps out to get you," he said.

"Yeah, you could say that," I said.

There were greens and yellows in flowery patterns.

"Clashes nicely though."

"Keep meaning to do it out," he said, "not into this decorating lark though. Don't s'pose you fancy yourself with a paint brush?"

"No," I said, "I don't."

"Didn't think so," he said, starting to organize mugs, tea-bags, and kettle.

I pointed at the muddy polystyrene dish on the draining board.

"What was that?"

"Chips and curry sauce," he said, "from the new place – it was good at the time – honest."

"Dare I ask when that was?" I said.

"Yesterday, no, day before."

"I'll take your word for it," I said, "but it looks like a museum exhibit to me."

He handed me a carton of milk.

"Taste that, see what it's like."

"You do it," I said.

"I hate sour milk," he said, "oh, all right, give it here then."

He sniffed it.

"I'd recommend it *without*," he said and poured it down the plug hole, semi solid. The smell was sharp and sickly.

"You're disgusting and it'll block," I said.

"I'm not and it won't," he said, "not if I run the hot water, blast it away."

He dropped the leftover take-away into the bin, the flap didn't open and so he kicked it. Then he picked up a cloth and wiped the table over. It was dull and covered in heat rings.

"Look at that," he said, winking, "good as new."

"At least," I said.

We'd always got on well – in our own way. Mucked around, had a laugh, usually at other people – the rest of the crowd – they were so *serious* sometimes. We'd do our double act, taking the piss until they gave in. Or until they'd had enough of us and got up and left.

I felt disappointed if he wasn't around. Wondered what he was doing, who he was with. He'd said, a couple of times, that I ought to come round – if I had nothing else to do. I didn't say no. I was waiting, hoping he'd say a particular night, then I'd know he really meant it.

I always thought something'd happen between us, eventually. But it's difficult to ask someone out. I thought maybe he was scared I'd turn him down, make him feel stupid. Still, now I was here. I felt chuffed.

He handed me the tea. Then introduced me to his two dead plants, Daphne and Delilah, and his pet stone.

"Don't touch it," he said, "it's that vicious – it'll have your arm off."

"Never mind that," I said, "I just hope you sterilized this mug. Or does it carry a health warning?"

"Come on," he said, "don't give me a hard time – or I'll shut you in the trunk, out the way."

"Ah, I noticed that thing," I said.

"That *thing*," he said, "charming. That *thing*'s an antique, y'know."

It stood to one side, old and weighty. The wood was scratched but somehow it managed to look good.

"What's in it?" I said.

"Only a few bits and pieces. And the body of the last person that hassled me," he said.

I lifted the lid. Turned over a couple of paperbacks that lay on top of the magazines and junk.

"Dammit. She must have escaped again," he said, raising his eyebrows and putting on his innocent expression – the one he always uses when he's talking trash. He was leaning against the wall, hands by his side, tapping his fingers against a patch of bare plaster. That's something else he does – taps his fingers, same old beat, one two three, one two three. Drives people mad, the more they complain, the more he does it to wind them up.

"Anyway, stop being nosey," he said, "come and sit down."

There was no space on the sofa, it was taken up with records and a defunct stereo system. We sat on the bed.

"One day," he said, "I'm gunna land myself a brilliant flat with all the gear in it – carpets up to me ankles, twin jacuzzi, robot to clean up . . ."

"That all?" I said.

"Well," he said, "I'd settle for anything that had two rooms – and a bathroom I didn't have to share with ten others. Be fine. But even that's out of reach."

"We could rob a bank," I said.

"Or marry millionaires," he said. "On second thoughts, no. Fed up with being judged on how much cash is in me pocket."

"Don't want to get married either," I said.

He smiled.

"You're not *aching* for a frilly dress and a string of bridesmaids then?"

I laughed.

"Well of course, if I tell the truth, I'm obviously en route to marriage, via the shortest possible road – I mean I'm bound to be, aren't I?"

"Now, now," he said, "we'll have less of the sarcasm. I know what you mean though."

"People seem to think there's something wrong with you if you don't want what they've settled for," I said.

"They want to know why, you mean – like there must be 'some reason'."

"And what if there is 'some reason'?" I said.

"Ah, but you forget, they're ignorant."

"Ignorance is no excuse," I said, "makes me sick."

"My old man says I'll 'come round' to getting hitched," he said.

"Well, I'm not saying I'll be on my own 'til the day I die," I said, "I'm saying I'll do what I want, when I want."

"Why not," he said, "do what you like. Who cares what anybody else thinks? I don't."

He paused, gulped his tea. I wasn't drinking mine, it was strong, I have it weak.

"Remember that time we all took off down the coast?" he said.

"Yeah, yeah," I said, "and my mother reported me missing to the police."

He laughed.

"That's right, yeah. You had no business being out that late, young lady."

"But what about when a certain person dived into the sea and cut his legs to pieces?"

"Don't change the subject," he said.

"Well all I can say is, thank God they never actually found me 'til I was home again," I said. "Would've been the embarrassment of all time."

"Wouldn't have locked you up or anything," he said, "not in a cell – maybe a playpen, but not a cell."

"Ha, ha," I said.

"Good laugh though," he said, "nobody seems to do anything any more."

"Should do," I said, "soon. Let's do something, say, next weekend?"

"Have to see," he said, shrugging.

"Or let's do something *now*."

"Such as?"

"I don't know."

"Bit limited I'm afraid, dear," he said, "unless you planned on terrorizing the neighbourhood or something, painting a few obscene slogans around town."

"Stupid," I said, "where were you going tonight anyway? Don't usually see you just wandering about the streets."

"Just wandering," he said, "sums it up."

"Pub out of favour now?"

"I went in for one," he said, "same old thing. Lenny telling me how I should've been there last night, had a great time, got smashed, had his head down the bog all night."

"*Great time*," I said.

"Lost his licence this week," he said, "definitely won't see him sober for the next year now."

"Anybody else about?"

"Not really," he said, "just Lenny and that, what's she called – girl with the long hair, you know?"

"Kim?" I said.

"That's it. Think she's gone back home with him."

"Rather her than me," I said.

"Let's phone him up," he said, "get him going."

"You've got a *phone*?" I said.

"Actually, that's why I said it. Knew you'd be impressed."

"We shouldn't *really*," I said.

"Come on," he said, "for a laugh."

It was on the floor with everything else. He lifted the receiver. Got a wrong number.

"Dunno who that was," he said, tried again, got it right. As soon as there was an answer from Lenny he hung up. Did it four or five times, trying not to give himself away.

"He'll be freaking out," he said.

"He'll get you back," I said.

"How's he gunna suss it's me," he said, "if he couldn't even spot a cop car tailing him for two miles?"

It amused him, and for some reason, me.

We talked about how Lenny'd been caught, sorted out, drunken drivers in general. Then football hooligans and muggers. Still left time for the last film we'd seen, the best and worst adverts on TV, who was working where and who wasn't working at all.

He leant over and pulled two cans of beer from under the bed, separated them.

"Forgot I had these left," he said, "definitely unchilled, but good enough."

"Tea and lager," I said.

"I know," he said, "I'm so sophisticated."

He shook his can, pointed it at me and pulled the ring. I ducked and the bitter foam sprayed a pile of clean T-shirts.

"Shit," he said, "didn't know you could move that fast."

"It'll give you something to do tomorrow," I said.

"Um," he said, and paused. "I lie here 'til lunchtime sometimes, trying to think of something to do."

"Slob," I said.

"*I am not.*"

"Thought you said you don't care what anyone thinks?"

"Yeah, well, I don't . . . all right, I get your point."

"What d'you do all day, really?" I said.

"I sit here," he said, "waiting for something to happen, only it never does."

He put his head in his hands and pretended to cry.

"Fool," I said.

"OK then, what about you?" he said.

"I make lists."

"Like?"

"Like, do washing, see if any post's arrived, buy newspaper."

He laughed.

"There's me cooped up here, waiting for my life to start, and you writing never-ending lists about nothing – p'raps we're both crazy."

He put his fingers up to his face making them into claws, hissed.

"Not funny though, is it?" he said.

"Maybe something'll turn up," I said, "work-wise I mean."

"Maybe," he said, "'til then, I'm on the outside, looking in."

We didn't speak for a while, he lay still, head buried in the duvet. It was past midnight and quiet.

I glanced up at some photos pinned to the wall, stretched to get a better view. They were old but I recognized a few faces that were still around.

Looked at the room again, properly. He was right I thought, about the chaos – it added

something rather than took anything away.
Without the clutter it'd just be a square, a cube,
a box.

There were books that I couldn't imagine him
reading. Music I couldn't imagine him playing.

It was shabby, but a bit like a kid's room in
ways. A cloth parrot on a perch, an inflatable
snake dangling from the ceiling.

He lifted himself onto his elbows and reached
for his drink.

"Still breathing then?" I said.

He sat up, swivelled round.

"OK – how many times d'you reckon your
average person breathes in, say, a year?" he said.

"Is this a joke?" I said.

"No. Come on. How many?"

"How should I know?"

"Work it out – minute, hour, day, year."

"Shut up," I said.

"I know," he said.

"How many then?"

"It's obviously . . . *a lot*."

I grabbed the pillow, threw it at him. He
caught it.

"Missed," he said, looking at me, grinning.
Kept looking, kept grinning.

"What you looking at?" I said.

"Seeing how many times you blink in a
minute."

"You're so *mature* sometimes," I said.

36

"There you go again," he said, "dead sarky."

"So?" I said.

"Well I was only *looking*." He said, "D'you know you've got funny eyes?"

"And what d'you mean by *funny*?" I said, covering them.

"Well, sort of, *funny*. Screwed up. Come here," he said, "let me see."

He put his hand under my chin to turn my head up to the light. The bulb was bright and bare.

"Get off," I said, "what d'you expect under that thing? It's like something from a spy movie."

"You've finally sussed me," he said, "I'm a secret agent. But if it's bothering you . . ."

He pulled the cord and the light went out.

"That better?" he said.

"Well, at least I can't see *you*," I said.

Just then, the telephone rang.

"*That bastard Lenny*," he said and let it ring.

Telling you, I feel like I should start defending myself here. Sounds like some gag – "What d'you do when you run out of conversation?" But it was my decision and I felt okay with it, nothing to do with anyone else.

At the same time, it was weird though. I had all these mad thoughts going through my mind. Like, what if the door bursts open and someone barges straight in, sees us? Or what if the house is burning down and I have to run out into the street, naked? He kept saying,

"Relax."

And I kept thinking,

"What if . . .?"

The sound of voices and traffic gradually got louder. I asked him if he was awake, he said he wasn't. The bed was pushed up against the window. I leant over, pulled the curtain back, looked out of the window. Daylight flooded in. He grunted in disapproval, covered his head with the sheet.

A woman in the room opposite was trying to get her son ready for school. He wouldn't stand still nor straight, she slapped him and he began to cry. The shop below them had opened its doors – a girl carried a board out to the front – "Cigs/milk/cold drinks/sandwiches". Workers dashed in and out, a few kids milled around. Occasionally someone would glance up, their eyes focusing on me for a split second.

"You going or staying?" he said. "Only whatever you're doing, put that bloody curtain back."

"I wonder where they're all going?" I said.

"Who?" he said.

"Them lot, out there."

"Who cares?" he said.

I dropped the curtain.

"Just a thought."

It was difficult to rest. Each time I moved, he tutted.

A quarrel started in the next flat.

"*I've had enough of this*," she shouted.

"And what d'you expect *me* to do about it?"

"*Anything*. But do *something*."

I asked him who they were.

"People," he said.

"D'you know them?" I said.

"Not really, they're just people. Ignore it."

"They always like this?"

"Why don't you go and ask them," he said, sighing.

I was uncomfortable. A door slammed, footsteps rained down the stairs.

I crawled out from under the covers, out of the sticky warmth into the cold. Began to dress. My shirt was crumpled on the ground, I pulled my jeans on, one sock was still in the leg, the other was missing.

"What time is it?" he said.

"Quarter past eight."

"What?" he said. "Can't be, not already."

He got up slowly, stretched, and gathered his clothes together.

"You off somewhere?" I said.

"Half past," he said, "moving me sister into a bedsit. Yet another dump."

He started dressing alongside me.

"Still, with any luck I won't have to put up with it for much longer," he said.

"Getting out?"

"Right out. May as well. Nothing here."

"S'pose not. Anywhere in mind?"

"Yeh. Well, not definite. But there must be loads of places better than here."

"When's this happening then?" I said.

"Not sure yet. Soon," he said.

He looked at the poster that'd fallen down from the wall.

"Soddin' thing," he said, "it's the damp."

The corners had torn. He tried to re-stick it with the same piece of tape, pressed his thumbs hard against it.

"What's the point?" he said, letting it drop again.

A horn blared outside.

"Shit – that'll be Chris," he said, "with the van."

He went to the window, put his hand up and mouthed five minutes. Then opened it and shouted, "I said – five minutes."

I stood in front of the mirror, brushing my hair. Looked a state. "Rats' tails", "burnt string" my mother used to say. Wasn't far wrong.

He laced his boots, searched for money, keys.

"Look, I gotta go," he said, "lock the door and that. I'll probably see you around, okay?"

"Probably," I said.

I put the brush down. Went over to the window, felt the breeze. Watched them in the street.

Chris had been on his way in, they'd met and were laughing.

"Average," he was saying.

"What's average?" Chris said.

"Well, I mean she wasn't bad," he said, "passable."

"'Member our shag-a-slag nights?" Chris said, and they laughed some more, before driving off.

There's no word for a male "slag" is there? Only congratulations. Funny that. Not that it makes me laugh.

On the Verge

"Carol, d'you ever wonder if you might be a lesbian?"

I chucked the words over my shoulder, concentrating the heat that rose in my body into pedalling my bike harder down the busy country road. We rode in single file because of the traffic, so I couldn't see her face. Neither could she see mine, I was glad about that.

It wasn't a question anyone talked about at school. But it was my secret fear and fantasy. I longed to know if other girls shared it, now was the moment of truth.

"Yes, sometimes. Do you?"

"Yeah." I paused, relief flooding through me made my heart beat faster.

"Does it bother you?" I'd slowed down now, because I kept looking over my shoulder at her.

"Well, it doesn't bother me, but there's not a lot of people I'd ever talk about it to 'cos they'd freak out. I just wonder sometimes what it would be like."

She spoke slowly, without embarrassment. Like the rest of her family she used few words, taking her time with them. She looked like a farmer's daughter, with her muscular arms, rosy face and masses of thick curly hair.

I'd grown up in a city, turning the pages of books instead of lifting hay bales. The early summer sun was already bringing out the freckles on my arms after our day on the road.

My father taught science at the polytechnic, my mum was taking some sort of psychology degree. In our family, everyone talked fast and constantly, arguing and pulling each other's ideas apart. They were pretty liberal in lots of ways, Dad was a communist before we were born. He made a lot of jokes about queers though, and my mum once said lesbians sent a shiver down her spine.

Anyway, now the subject was out at last, I wasn't about to let it drop. I turned down the next lane we came to on the left. It was high hedged and quiet. A little way down was a crossroads, the signpost on a triangle of grass in the middle. I got off my bike and let it fall to the ground.

"Let's have our sandwiches here, shall we?"

We got out the food we'd made that morning, and for a while we just sat and ate in silence. I felt a bit light-headed with excitement. Carol hadn't giggled, or cycled off in disgust to tell everyone I was a pervert. She was sitting beside me peeling an orange. We'd started to get to know each other that year at school, going round in the same crowd.

"It's not just wondering what it would be like in bed. What do they do the rest of the time? Have you ever met a lesbian?"

"Everyone said Miss Walker was one, behind her back I mean. She was a games teacher, before you came here. She had a motorbike. You could see she was dead lonely. Anyway, she got a job in London and left."

I watched Miss Walker as she roared off towards the city, until she was just a cloud of dust, wondered how she was getting on.

"There are clubs and stuff in cities. I saw one in a film. Half the women were dressed as men with their hair greased back, the rest were got up like Cindy dolls. They were really horrible to each other, getting drunk and playing mind games. Mental. I think most of them were dead by the end."

The images in the film had disturbed me. Carol laughed though.

"Well, they're bound to make it like that in films, aren't they? Miss Walker didn't play mind games, she was really nice. If anything was bothering you, she'd tell you to go and run it off! She was the fittest woman I've ever seen!"

We both laughed. It felt wonderful, talking over these dead of night topics in the afternoon sun. We lay there in the long grass for ages, talking and talking on and on.

"It must be awful to feel such an outcast from society. And people saying it's because they can't get a man. Maybe they can't anyway. Sometimes I wonder if I give off some sort of special lesbian scent. Perhaps everybody, boys, sort of sense it on me. Maybe that's why no one ever asks me out."

This was another of my late night fantasies that had never before seen the light of day. Painfully serious, I looked into her eyes for a reaction. She stared back for a moment, then creased up laughing.

"Lesbian scent!" she chuckled, shaking her head.

I'd been about to get offended, but realizing how daft it sounded, I joined in.

"Who do you want to ask you out anyway? They're all such morons if you ask me."

"Well, no one in particular. I just want to know what it's like."

"You will do one day. I'm not staying round here for ever."

"But I want to know now. I'll be sixteen soon. I'm still a virgin and I just want to get on with it, so I know."

"You worry too much. Would you rather be like Sarah? She's probably round at her place, hand in hand with Martin at this very moment."

Sarah's this girl we know who is always going out with someone. She and Martin have been a steady number for a few months, they spend break and lunch times glued together.

"What the hell do they talk about, that's what I want to know. I can't imagine talking like this with a bloke, can you?"

"You must be joking. They're always too busy showing themselves off. Martin was moaning on to me on the bus the other day, about Sarah, and how she's too possessive and all that. But the minute we got in, he went straight off to find her. He just wanted to appear the coolest."

"Yuk, what a wanker."

"Anyway, they probably don't do much talking. I expect they spend most of their time with their lips otherwise engaged!"

She got up, shaking the pollen out of her clothes.

"I'll have to be back soon. Ride as far as Harberton with me and we can get an ice-cream."

When I got home, Mum was sitting in the garden, talking and drinking with a friend from college.

"Hallo, darling. There's some potatoes in the oven and a salad on the side. Everyone's had some except Eva, so leave a bit for her. Did you have a good time? Good! Go on then. I'll be in later when we've finished." She said it all in one breath, then turned straight back to her conversation. I went round the house and into the kitchen.

My sister Eva and my dad were nowhere to be seen. Robert, my younger brother, was at the table reading a skateboard magazine. He stuck his leg out in front of me and we had a quick tussle, by way of saying hallo. I went over to investigate the food.

"Look at these wheels, Anna. I'm going to get a set of these in three weeks. They're Kryptonite, listen . . ."

He read out a technical description of the wheels. I listened, trying to pick up on whatever it was that got him so excited and kept him poring over these adverts for weeks. But soon my mind wandered, turning over the word Kryptonite, and the chunky green and red plastics in the picture while he reeled off sizes and prices . . .

"Any food left? I'm starving!" Eva burst through the door. She made a beeline for the food, filled a plate in about twenty seconds, and sat down to eat. She did everything fast and efficiently, her earrings swinging and clinking together as she took small, sharp bites of food. She was seventeen, the lead singer in a band. Her problems were to do with too many drooling men hanging around her. By comparison I felt slow and dull, so on the whole I kept my life and friends separate. She seemed to prefer it that way too, so I was surprised when she said:

"Adam Rogers is having a party in his barn on Saturday. He said you can come if you want, as long as you don't tell all your lot and they turn up and be sick everywhere."

"He was pretty sick himself at your party. I might come though, I'll tell Carol about it. How come he's asking us then?"

"I dunno. There's probably too many blokes going and he's trying to even it out."

She finished her salad as she spoke, running her finger quickly round the plate and licking it clean. She tossed the plate in the sink and disappeared upstairs.

I followed more slowly and went into my room. Since my bed stuck out into the middle of the room, the underneath was not a safe place to hide things. I lay across it and lifted the corner of the carpet behind to get at the school jotter I used as a diary. I wrote about the day I'd spent with Carol, how close I felt with her. For the first time the idea occurred to me that I could have reached out and kissed her, we could have spent the afternoon lying in each other's arms.

I'd arranged to meet Carol first thing Monday morning behind the sports hall, where we smoked. Coming round the corner I came across some of the boys playing poker dice on the ground. Martin's bum was sticking straight out in front of me, so I gave it a pinch as I passed. He leapt forward, then turned bright red.

"Morning, Martin. It looked so tempting I just couldn't resist!"

The other boys laughed at his blushes. Sarah, leaning against the wall in the background, rolled her eyes at me.

"Honestly, Anna, you are awful."

"Oh well, you should be grateful. Now you've got an excuse to kiss it better later on." I said, lighting up a cigarette. It irritated me that she was so easily shockable.

Carol turned up a few minutes later, but Sarah collared her first and began an intense whispered conversation in the corner. There was something about Carol that inspired everyone to confide in her. Girls and boys alike told her their most juicy bits and pieces. This looked pretty interesting, so I left them to it and went into school. I knew she'd fill me in as soon as we were alone.

We met up again at lunchtime and walked into town, settling down for the afternoon at our favourite table, tucked away round the corner in a cafe. We had £1.20 and six fags. Rationed carefully, this would see us through to 3.30 when Carol had to catch the school bus home.

"Well, guess what?" she said once we'd got ourselves some tea.

"You're running away to join Miss Walker's all girl motorbike gang."

"Yeah, that's right. How did you know?"

"No, I give up. Something to do with Sarah?"

"Yes. They did it. Her and Martin, that's what all that whispering was about."

"God, really? This weekend?"

"Yeah. In the woods by her house. She was full of it, I can tell you. She said it's changed everything, that the whole world looks different, though she couldn't describe how. She said I'd have to try it myself to really understand."

I listened avidly, feeling totally jealous that Sarah had experienced this mysterious transformation. She'd passed into a world we knew nothing about, unless you counted a few groping sessions at parties.

"They have been together for ages, Anna. I mean, I know they're a pain in the arse, but they do care for each other."

"Oh I know. But I just can't stand it. She's smug enough as it is, now she'll be unbearable. Thinking she's a woman and we're mere girls."

"Who cares what she thinks? You don't even like her."

"It's not about her really. It's what I think. And I swear to God, Carol, if no one asks me soon, I'm going to bloody well ask somebody myself!"

"For Christ's sake! One day you're wondering

whether you're a lesbian, then the next you're ready to proposition any old bloke for a quick screw. I reckon you're just obsessed with sex. Why don't you go and ask him?" She nodded towards a middle-aged man, with bits of dandruff on his lapels, bent over a newspaper.

"Fuck off!" I said, kicking her under the table. "Listen though. There's a party at Adam Rogers's place on Saturday. D'you fancy coming with me? Maybe I'll ask someone there."

"I don't believe you would."

I pretended to look sophisticated at her over the table, dragging deeply on a cigarette. She took it off me and finished it herself.

"I can't come. I won't be here. We're going to my aunt's in Bristol this weekend, for my grand-parents' wedding anniversary."

"Mmmm. That sounds wild."

"Oh, it'll be OK. Cath, my cousin, is really nice. She said she'd take me out to a club on Saturday."

"Well, I'm going to go to this party, and on Monday I'll tell you if the world looks different and everything is utterly changed!"

"Just be careful, Anna. Don't do anything stupid."

Lying in the bath on Saturday night, I wondered what Carol was up to in Bristol, wished she was with me getting ready, like she usually was before a party. Even Eva wasn't going to be there now, she'd disappeared off to London to stay with her boyfriend. But the fact that I was on my own made it easier to get in the mood for what I was planning to do. Carol would have talked me out of it, and I'd have been too embarrassed in front of Eva. Drying myself in front of the mirror I saw alternating images; me the raunchy young daredevil would suddenly be replaced by me with anxious eyes, surveying my pale body disdainfully. I left the mirror, got dressed in familiar jeans, red tracksuit top and my baseball boots. I spiked up my hair, then went downstairs.

Dad looked up from *The Times* crossword and smiled at me.

"You look nice, chick. Doesn't she look lovely, Marion, mmm?"

Mum glanced up from what she was doing at the cooker and nodded absently.

"I don't know why you have to wear those jeans *all* the time though. You've got plenty of other things up there."

I didn't want all this attention, I was feeling self-conscious enough as it was. I put on my jacket.

"I'll see you later then. Are you staying in?"

"Yes. Dave and Joyce are coming to dinner, so don't bring a lot of people back with you. Are you going to the pub?"

"Yeah. Then a party. See you!"

It was still light as I walked to the pub. The pavements were covered in slugs and silvery slug trails, millions of them, on the move for mating purposes probably. Quite a few had got squashed and were dried up and stuck to the concrete. It was the same every year.

The pub was packed. The town was of a size that only one pub at a time could be *the* place to go. Every few months the venue changed, and all the mixed band of drama students, hippies, bikers in leather, and the school pupils like me who made up at least half the customers, would up and flood the back bar of somewhere new. In this way the profits, and the hassle with underage drinkers and dope smoking in the bar, were spread out between the town's landlords.

I got myself a drink, then sussed out a lift to the party with some of Eva's friends, four of the seven hippies who lived in a disused watermill outside town. Two of the blokes were discussing the news from South Africa.

". . . but killing other blacks, it's dog eat dog. I can't see that violence is going to get them anywhere."

"If people are colluding with the state their colour is irrelevant, they must be taught that what they're doing is unacceptable."

"Maybe they don't care what sort of impression they're making on you. Maybe they're just really angry." I sat down at their table and introduced myself into the argument.

"Well, without international pressure, the white government will carry on regardless, so it's foolish to dismiss world opinion."

"How long do you think people can carry on being on their best behaviour with no one taking any notice? Violence is what gets on the news . . ."

The discussion continued in the car and all the way to the party. I was enjoying myself, and it wasn't till I'd been in the barn some time that I remembered my mission. Quite drunk by this time, I looked around. A few couples were dancing, mostly people were sitting on hay bales that ringed the room. There were more blokes than girls, in gangs of four or five, drinking and shoving each other and grinning all the time to show they were enjoying themselves. At one end of the room I spotted Tony, whose brother Steven I went round with at school. I'd met Tony at their house and he'd always been friendly. I'd never fancied him, but sitting there staring in front of him with a beer bottle in his lap he looked clean and relaxed. When I sat down next to him he looked up and grinned.

"All right, Anna? How's it going? Having a good time?"

"Yeah, not bad. I don't know many people here."

"Where's Eva? Didn't you come with her?"

"She's up in London. I came with that lot in their car. But I'm on a personal mission."

"Uh huh," his gaze had strayed back to the dance floor. "What sort of mission?"

"My mission is, that before this night is through, I will be rid of my virginity for ever."

I said it in the same chit-chatty tone as the rest of the conversation. My toes curled tight at how bald it sounded. He turned round and stared at me. He was drunk too, I think he was wondering if I was serious. As I stared back, he shook his head from side to side, then started laughing. The laugh became a roar, and when he sat up to gasp for breath he lost his balance and toppled backwards off the bale onto the wooden floor. It was pretty funny. I was laughing myself as he crawled back on his seat, giggling weakly.

"Oh dear! Well I've never heard a girl say that before. You're crazy, Anna, mad. A mission . . ." he chuckled again.

"As a matter of fact, I came over here to ask you."

"What? To ask me to deflower you? Oh Jesus, Anna, leave it out. If you want to know, I've not done it myself yet, and when I do I'll be the one doing the asking."

"That's very sexist of you."

"I don't give a shit. Anyway, I don't find being

55

propositioned by one of Steven's friends very sexy, so forget it. See you later."

With that he got up and disappeared. I lit a cigarette and hoped no one nearby had overheard all that. Oh well, what the hell, I thought, it's a bit late to worry now. I drained my glass and went to look for another drink. It was for real now, and there was no way I was going to leave it at that now I'd started. My pride wouldn't let me, severely dented as it was. Practice, I told myself rooting for a bottle opener, that was a practice run. Drink in hand, I leaned back against the wall.

"Hallo, Anna. How are you these days?"

Standing right next to me was John, a friend of Eva's boyfriend from London. I knew him fairly well, he'd stayed at our house a few weeks the summer before. I grinned.

"John. Hallo. Where did you spring from?"

"I came down today. I've got a job in Dartmouth for the summer. How's the family?"

"Oh, they're all right. Doing the usual sort of things. Eva's up at Micky's, everyone else is at home."

"Yeah. I saw Eva last night. She and Mick are flying to New York in the morning. Don't tell anyone though, it's a secret at the moment."

"God, really? Tomorrow. Mum's going to go mad. She's got her exams soon. Has she told them yet?"

"I think she's going to ring them tomorrow, when it's too late for them to do anything."

He knew our parents, so he had some idea of the reaction they were going to have to Eva leaving the country just before her "A" levels. I stood there thinking about Eva for a while, jetting off to America with her man, getting off on the romance of it all. Then I remembered my mission.

"John," he looked up from rolling a cigarette, "would you like to deflower me tonight?"

He raised his eyebrows, but didn't laugh. Licked and stuck the cigarette, then lit it.

"Yes, all right then, it would be my pleasure. Shall we go?"

"Yes, now. Let's go now."

I followed him out to where his bike was parked, suddenly not feeling drunk any more. Riding along in the cold night air I played the girl on the back of the motorbike, bending dramatically into the corners. Too soon he stopped at the end of our garden. I hadn't even considered what my parents might say. My plan had only gone as far as the propositioning. As it turned out they were safely settled in the back garden, drinking brandy and talking loudly with the Mitchells. We went up to my room.

It was all happening very quickly. I left the light off and got undressed. Putting my watch on the shelf I had a moment's panic, wished I wasn't doing this. But he was getting undressed behind me and soon we were lying naked against each other in my single bed. We started kissing and stuff, and I began to get into it. Very quickly it seemed, he got on top of me, and was pushing his erection in the direction of my small, dry vagina.

"Relax, just relax," he said rather frantically. I looked at the familiar print of my duvet cover over his shoulder and tried to move into a better position. When he found his way inside me it felt uncomfortable and tight. I felt removed inside from what I was doing. He came quickly, and rolled off me. Not a moment too soon as it turned out. There were footsteps coming up the stairs. Footsteps I knew well.

"Shit! Mum's coming. Hide!"

In the few seconds it took for her to open the door and switch on the light, he rolled off the bed onto the floor behind. Her head appeared as his leg disappeared behind me.

"Anna, are you . . . Oh, sorry," and with that she closed the door again. That was the last thing I expected her to do, but I think she was too surprised to do anything else for the time being. John was on his feet in a moment, struggling into his trousers.

"I don't believe it! She'll kill me. She never liked me anyway."

"It's all right, she's gone."

"She'll be back in a minute when she realizes what she saw, and I don't want to be here when she does! Listen, I'm gonna climb out the window."

"Don't be stupid, you'll break your neck!"

"The living room window, I don't want to meet her on the way out. Look, do us a favour, push my bike to the end of the lane and I'll meet you there."

I couldn't help laughing as I watched him clamber out the window, then hare off in a big circle through the neighbours' garden. The drama of this turn of events was quite to my liking. Leaving through the kitchen door, I went out and pushed the heavy bike up the lane. He came puffing up a few minutes later.

"Thanks, Anna. Look, I'll see you around, OK. I just hope she didn't see my face."

"Are you really scared of her?"

"Definitely. I'm off!"

He kissed me on the cheek, started the bike and drove away. As the noise of his engine faded into the distance it became very quiet for the first time in hours. I stood there in the dark for a while before going inside and back up to my room. Apart from the unfamiliar smell of my bed, and a rawness between my legs the world looked just the same as always. I fell asleep expecting Mum to burst through the door at any moment.

* * *

She didn't though. By the time I got up the next morning Eva had rung and dropped her bombshell about America and Mum had gone out. She'd obviously found time to tell my dad though.

"I hope you're using some form of contraception," he said pompously, as I passed him on my way to the bathroom.

I felt fragile all day and wandered round the house in a bit of a daze. When Mum got back in the afternoon I was making a chocolate cake. She filled me in about Eva.

". . . and then there's you. What was all that about last night? Are you going out with him?"

"No, I'm not, I just wanted to see what it was like, that's all."

"And. What was it like?"

I shrugged. "All right. I don't know really. Anyway, he ran off the moment we'd finished." I licked the cake mixture off the spoon.

"Oh Anna, look. It's totally different when you love someone, a totally different experience. Just get on with other things and wait till you meet somebody you really like. Sex is given far too much importance these days. There are plenty of other things: You could be writing, or reading, anything instead of getting screwed by a loser like that."

"Maybe I'm just not into men," I said recklessly, "maybe I never will be."

"Don't be ridiculous. There are lots of very nice men around, you'll just have to wait."

We didn't speak of it again after that, she could probably see I wasn't about to do it again in a hurry. I ate most of the cake and went to bed early. I was exhausted, and impatient for the morning when I could see Carol and tell her all about it.

I was in the bus bay at half past eight. Seeing Steven get off one bus brought back the first part of the party with a flush. I stuck out my chin and glared at him when he passed, daring him to say anything. He just nodded and went straight past. Maybe Tony didn't tell him.

Carol looked lovely when she jumped off her bus a few minutes later. She had her hair tied back with a red and white bandana, and her eyes were sparkling. She grinned when she saw me.

"Hallo. I'm glad you're early for a change. I've got millions to tell you. Let's go and have a fag." She took my arm. "I was going to ring you last night, but we didn't get back till late. Listen, you've got to come up there with me. Cath's really into it, she's got the top floor of the house to herself. And Anna, you'll never guess what . . ." She looked at me, then stopped. "What's up with you? Did you have a bad weekend? Did you go to that party?"

I nodded, and looked at her wordlessly. She got the idea.

"You did it, didn't you? Oh God, this is all too much. We'd better take the morning off and go down in the woods. But I just must tell you."

"What?"

"Cath's a lesbian."

"She's not!"

"She is! She has been for about a year. And there are loads of them. I met all her mates at this women's disco on Saturday. They were really nice, Anna. No one was dressed up as a bloke. Some of them were our age. I've got this paper they're printing in my bag for you. Cath and Bel got it together mostly. Bel did the illustrations."

"Who's Bel?"

Carol grinned. "She's Cath's best friend. I really liked her. She gave me this scarf."

My weekend started to seem quite insignificant in the face of all this. I stared at her smiling face.

"We went for a walk together yesterday. I've never felt like this about anybody before."

"Carol! I can't believe it."

"I don't care what you think. I like her, and I really liked kissing her."

"You kissed? Tell me about it from the beginning."

By this time we had crossed the playing field and disappeared into the shade of the woods. Our spot was a pipe that spanned a little stream.

We sat there with our legs dangling and she told me about her weekend. Then I told her about mine. She cracked up at the funny bits, but she squeezed my hand as well.

". . . so it was pretty awful all in all," I ended up.

"Oh well. At least you've done it now. I mean, maybe you'll take it a bit easier now, not feel so desperate, now you know what it's like."

"Don't worry, I'm not planning on doing anything like that again in a hurry! You sound a bit like my mum, 'just you wait for the right man to come along'."

"Or the right woman! Listen, come to Bristol with me in a couple of weeks. You'll love it, there's so much going on. It'll cheer you up. Will you?"

"Yes. I'd like to, it sounds really good. And now give me a fag. We'll have to be back soon. I've got Mrs Benson after break, and you know what she's like on a Monday."

A Long Ride on the Carousel

Last summer, I learned about love from Mr Fuller. It's not what you're thinking. That part of love, the physical part, is easy, compared with what Mr Fuller taught me. At first, I thought I'd write to Simon Bates and try to get on "Our Tune", on Radio One, but I could never fit everything into the time: the feelings and the place and the people. So I'm writing it straight out, however long it takes.

I live in Seatown, which is a holiday resort. Seatown isn't its real name, and I'm not really Shirley, and all the other names that appear are made up by me. Apart from that, everything else is true.

The good thing about living in a seaside town is that you always know of someone who runs a boarding house or small hotel or B and B and who needs a hand during the season. Last July, I went to work the day school ended. Mrs Beecham's hotel was called The Abercrombie. There was another girl working there as well. Her name was Lorna. The Abercrombie was quite big: seven tables in the dining room and a little bar behind the desk and a TV lounge upstairs on the first floor. It was fairly clean. All the tablecloths were reasonably white and the lace curtains a lot less dingy than some I'd seen. Mrs Beecham kept the notices on the green baize board quite up-to-date. I only found one from the year before, drawing the attention of guests to the coronation of Seatown's Flower Queen.

The carpets throughout the hotel were a pattern of brown and orange whirlpools.

"I like a bit of colour," was one of the things Mrs Beecham was fond of saying, and there was a fair amount of it about in The Abercrombie, one way or another. Apart from the orange whirlpool carpets, there was rose-trellis wallpaper in the bedrooms in a couple of dozen shades of mauve and purple and pink. The bathrooms had unnaturally blue shower curtains the colour of swimming-pool water. At suppertime (6.00 p.m. to 7.30 p.m. Monday to Friday, 6.30 p.m. to 8.00 p.m. Saturday and Sunday) we served a different coloured soup each night, ranging from a tomato which almost matched the carpet, through beige mushroom, yellowish chicken, pale green leek, and dark brown minestrone to the glorious emerald of pea and bacon.

Lorna and I had our work cut out. There's plenty to do in a hotel, I can promise you. Beds to be made and covered up with candlewick bedspreads (fluffy yellow), loo rolls to check, tables to be cleared from breakfast and made up again with knives and forks etc ready for supper, cans of soup to be opened, the bar to be wiped down, the china ladies in crinoline dresses on the mantelpiece of the TV lounge to be dusted – it was never-ending. We hardly had a spare minute during the day and by the time evening came, we were generally too exhausted to do more than collapse on one of the shiny plastic seats of the Western Grill 'n' Griddle, across the road from The Abercrombie.

I didn't mind any of it. I loved it. I was happy, walking about on Cloud 9. The reason for this was Adam. Adam was my boyfriend. He was the first proper boyfriend I'd ever had, and nothing Mrs Beecham could throw at me could take the shine off my romance. And it *was* romantic, the way I'd met him. All my friends thought it was, and Lorna thought so too, when I told her. It happened like this.

Seatown's main Promenade, which stretches from the Fairground at one end to the Leisure Complex at the other, is just one long line of hotels and shops selling plastic shoes, sticks of rock, horrible T-shirts and animals made of shells. Also mugs with "A gift from Seatown" printed on them. Every now and then there's an amusement arcade or a shooting gallery or a bingo place and, dotted all along the Prom, there are kiosks selling candy floss and soggy, grey burgers and limp sausages in stale buns. I try and keep away from it most of the time, but this day, the day I met Adam, I was walking along it for some reason. Every time I *did* go along the Prom, I always used to stop and look at two things. I couldn't help it. They fascinated me in the way that a chamber of horrors fascinates some people. They don't want to look, they *have* to look. What drew me, every time, was two life-size moving dummies in glass cases: Grandma Clampitt and the Laughing Clown. With the Laughing Clown (orange nylon hair, purple and white striped suit, huge lips the colour of blood in a chalk-white face) you had to put 10p in a slot, and then he would move, rock backwards and forwards and from side to side, while the rattle and grind of metal laughter filled the air. Children seemed to love it. Coin after coin would fall into the slot. I never put any money in, although perhaps I should have done. If the Laughing Clown was menacing when he moved, he was positively evil when he didn't. I had the feeling, even when there was no one about to put a 10p in, that he was just about to start moving as I passed his glass case. Crazy, right? Grandma Clampitt was even worse. She was an old lady in a long red and white gingham dress, sitting on a rocking chair with a rifle held across her knees. She had white hair in a bun and ice-coloured eyes. She was in a case just outside a shooting gallery and with her you didn't even need 10p.

She would shudder into movement all by herself, worked by some kind of remote control. What she did was try and entice you in to have a go yourself with the guns and the targets.

"Come on, y'all," she'd say in a voice like old razor-blades. "It sho' is a whole lotta fun. Step right up, folks!" Then her chair would start rocking and rocking and the ice-coloured eyes would glitter as they caught the light of the neon sign above the glass case.

Anyway, one day I was looking at Grandma Clampitt and this yobbo starts on me. You know: hello darling, come and have a go with me then I'll buy you a Coke, any more at home like you . . . you know the kind of thing. He was horrible. I didn't even need to look at him to see he was horrible, and I turned as quickly as I could and tried to walk away, and then he put his hand on my arm, and tried to pull me back towards him. I nearly died. I couldn't think what to do. I wanted to scream and kick him and run away, but there's always another part of you that says: don't make a fuss, don't shout, don't draw attention to yourself. I couldn't move. I was paralysed. In the end I pulled my arm away and he pulled it back, exactly as if I were a rag-doll. Then I heard someone say:

"Doesn't look like she wants to go with you, does it, mate?" and like magic the horrible greasy hand left my arm. I turned and saw Adam. I could understand why the creep had disappeared. Adam was well over six feet tall and dressed in black from head to toe. He looked to me like a kind of angelic deliverer. I burst into tears.

"Hey!" he said. "What's all this then? Haven't I just rescued you?"

"That's what I'm crying about," I said. "It's pathetic, needing to be rescued. I should be able to look after myself. I bet you think I'm a prize divvy."

"No, I don't. I just think you're not used to things like that happening . . . or to nerds like him. If I hadn't come along, you'd have kicked him in the end."

"I didn't want to make a fuss, though."

"That's stupid. Promise me you won't care about that in future. That's really stupid."

"OK," I said. "I promise."

"You look as if you could do with a coffee, or something," he said. "My name's Adam. What's yours?"

"Shirley."

We went round the corner and had a coffee in the Western Grill 'n' Griddle – yes, the very same . . . the one opposite The Abercrombie Hotel.

After that night, when I was so soppily and romantically rescued by my knight in black denim from the clutches of the dastardly villain on the Prom I saw Adam almost every day. One

69

thing, as they say, led to another and in forty-eight hours I was in love. I thought about him every single minute. When I was with him, I couldn't let go his hand, couldn't tear my eyes away from him. I dreamed about him, went over our conversations again and again, felt myself flying into a million separate shining pieces every time he kissed me – I don't have to tell you. You know the sort of thing I mean. It's embarrassing to go into it in too much detail. The night Adam rescued me was May 13th. I started working at Mrs Beecham's on July 24th: six weeks or so of Paradise.

I saw less of Adam once I started work. He had a summer job too. We discussed it, and we both agreed that it would be good to have the extra money. Perhaps, we said, if we collected enough between us, we could go on holiday together next year, somewhere far away from the flabby hot dogs and the smell of yesterday's fried onions.

Then one day about the middle of August, Mr Fuller arrived at The Abercrombie. I noticed him straight away, the very first time he came down to breakfast, because he was so different from the usual guests. I find it hard to tell people's ages, but he looked to me about seventy. He had white hair, and a longish face which seemed to have grooves cut into it. He wore a grey, three-piece suit, as though he weren't on holiday at all, but off to work in a bank or an office somewhere. As if that weren't strange enough, he always carried a plastic shopping bag around with him, whenever I saw him. The other thing that was remarkable about Mr Fuller was that he realized you were a person. Most visitors acted as though Lorna and I were invisible. Well, in my case, maybe that's just possible. I'm not exactly startling, but Lorna with her mane of red curls and her turquoise eyes – you'd have to be blind not to see her. Still, an absent "Ta very much" was all we ever got from most people, with never so much as a glance in our direction. Mr Fuller spoke to us and took an interest in our answers.

"I'm sure I'm right in thinking," he said to me one day, "that this is just a holiday job."

"Oh, yes," I said. "I'm going to be a TV camera man. I mean camera woman."

"Nowadays," he said, smiling at me, "you're supposed to say 'camera person'."

I liked him. I liked the way he took me seriously and joked with me at the same time. He even took the trouble to ask me what my name was. For the first three days of his stay, he vanished after breakfast, and only returned at suppertime to eat his colourful soup. I wondered, as I tidied his room, where he went and what he did, holding his plastic bag. All his personal stuff must have been in there, because his clothes and toilet things were all there was in his room. There was nothing that told you anything about him. His belongings could have been anyone's.

Lorna and I had different afternoons off. Mine was Wednesday, hers was Thursday. On this particular Wednesday, I had arranged to meet Adam at the Fairground. He liked all those things; the Waltzer, the Roller Coaster, and especially the Carousel, with all the golden horses going round and round and up and down to the jangly music that was like no other music in the world. Just before I was about to set out to meet him, he rang me. He couldn't make it. There was a panic on at his hotel . . . never mind. I went to the Fairground by myself in a foggy, nostalgic mood. It was a lovely day, one of the few sunny days of last summer. I wandered around, happily enough and eventually I ended up where I always ended up: beside the painted horses. I was looking at them going round and round and then I saw him: Mr Fuller was riding the Carousel in his three-piece grey suit and hugging his plastic shopping bag. Round and round he went, with the laughter and shrieks of the children on the other horses flying in the air around him. He stared straight in front of him, not seeing anything, not seeing me. I didn't want him to see me. I felt as though I'd caught him doing something embarrassing, something shameful. As the Carousel slowed down, I walked away. When I turned back to look, he was paying the man for another ride. He hadn't even got off his horse.

That evening, even though it was my day off, I'd agreed to help behind the bar. Mr Fuller was sitting alone at one of the little tables with a bowl of peanuts in front of him. He'd arranged a few of them in a circle, pushing them carefully with the tip of one finger till they were where he wanted them to be. I don't know what got into me then, why I said what I did. I went over, and before I could stop myself, the words came out:

"I saw you today, you know. Going round on the Carousel."

He smiled. "Good evening, Shirley. Why don't you sit down for a moment?"

I sat down on a small stool covered in crimson plush. I thought he wasn't going to say any more about it, but he did.

"Yes, the Carousel. I've always liked it. I go there every afternoon. We came to Seatown on our honeymoon, my wife and I. Of course, that was a long time ago. Everything was different then. Quite different."

I didn't stop to think. I should have. I mean, I could see how old Mr Fuller was . . . the possibility should have occurred to me. I said:

"Why have you come on your holidays all by yourself, then?"

"Because my wife is dead," he answered and if I could have disappeared into one of the orange whirlpools on the carpet, I would have done, that very minute.

"I'm sorry," I muttered, "I should have thought. I *am* sorry, honestly."

Mr Fuller smiled. "It's perfectly all right. She is better, far better, being dead. She is at peace. I know, you see, because I killed her."

I think I must have turned white or red or both, because he went on:

"There's no need to be alarmed. I am not, in the usual sense, a murderer. We made the plan together. We are old. She was dying. She couldn't bear the pain, and I couldn't bear to see her suffering. I could not watch the disease unfolding new shoots in her body every day." He took two peanuts from the dish and placed them right in the centre of the circle made by the other peanuts. Then he looked up at me. I noticed for the first time (because I never look at old people, not properly) how blue his eyes were, how young-looking, how bright. He looked straight at me and said:

"I loved her very much, you see."

"Yes," I said lamely.

"On our honeymoon," Mr Fuller continued, "we used to ride the Carousel. 'Do you love me?' she'd ask. And I'd say: 'As long as the music goes round.' People say the daftest things on their honeymoons . . . 'As long as the music goes round' . . . and round and round we'd go." He ate a peanut. "Of course, it was all much cheaper then, going on the rides."

I nodded. Mr Fuller took a sip of his beer. "She said it to me again, that last night. 'Do you love me?' she said. And I said: 'As long as the music goes round.' That's what I said to her, and I meant it. 'Then let me go to sleep,' she said, 'and finish with all this hurting.' So I did. I let her go to sleep. I dressed her in her best nightie and gave her drinking chocolate. I crushed all her sleeping pills into it and an extra spoon of sugar so that it shouldn't be too bitter for her." He looked up at me and then saw that I was crying.

"I'm sorry," he said. "I shouldn't have said anything. I've gone and upset you now. Don't be sad. I'm not sad. We had over fifty years together. A long ride on the Carousel. She's not in pain any more. I like to think of her like that: not hurting." He finished his drink and stood up.

"Cheer up, Shirley. It'll all seem different tomorrow." I smiled weakly as he left the room, carrying his shopping bag.

The next day when I arrived at The Abercrombie, there was a police car outside, which pulled away and vanished round the corner in a screech of rubber as I opened the door. I found Mrs Beecham in the kitchen, in a tizzy. It was hard to piece together what she was saying because it was all coming out in such a jumble, but I got the message soon enough. Mr Fuller was dead. The police had found him on a bench near the Leisure Complex, with his shopping bag beside him. There was a Thermos flask, too. The police were analysing the contents. There was a note explaining that he had decided to end his own life, and another to Mrs Beecham with money in it for his bill and an apology for any upset.

". . . and I must say," said Mrs Beecham, "it was considerate of him not to die in the hotel. Word does get round about that kind of thing, you know. It wouldn't be good for business, no indeed. Shirley, will you come with me and pack his belongings? The police will be calling for them later."

I followed her upstairs. I thought: these shirts, this Paisley scarf, this toothbrush, they aren't Mr Fuller. He's with his wife, I said to myself, comforting myself like a child. I didn't believe it in my heart of hearts, but I wanted to. I closed my eyes and forced a picture into my head of Mr Fuller and a pretty lady with white hair sitting together in a small room, on either side of a fireplace . . . of Mr Fuller and his bride like Adam and me, going round and round on the golden fairground horses. These pictures kept dissolving into tears. I stripped the bed and rolled the sheets and pillowcases into a bundle for the wash.

Over the next few weeks, I thought about Mr Fuller sometimes, but less and less each day, until by about the beginning of September, he had disappeared almost completely from my thoughts.

Then, one Thursday, Mrs Beecham asked me would I mind giving a hand in the bar that evening, after supper. I could have an hour or so off in the afternoon instead, even though it wasn't strictly my day off, but Lorna's. Yes, I said, and went off along the Prom. There's no easy way of saying what happened next. I caught sight of Lorna's red hair a little way ahead of me, so I ran to catch up with her. I stopped almost immediately. Adam was with her, next to her, and just so that there should be nothing left unclear or shadowy, his arm was around her waist and she was leaning into his body as though she intended to grow into him. Not a thing you've heard or read or seen prepares you for what it feels like. Every single thing about the world and you in it feels wrong, feels bad. Every surface of your body is raw. I'm not proud of what I did after that. I followed them without them seeing me. I watched them walk into the Fairground. I saw them squeezed together in to a round blue metal container on the Waltzer, but I turned away when he kissed her because I couldn't bear it. I don't know how I found my way back to The Abercrombie, but I did. I walked through the rest of the evening like a zombie, holding the pain somewhere right at the centre of me, where no one else could see it. I was supposed to meet Adam in the Western Grill 'n' Griddle after work. All evening I'd been thinking: I won't go. I'll run away. I never want to see him again . . . but by the time work finished, I'd changed my mind.

He was there when I arrived. He waved at me.

"Hi . . . I've got a Coke for you,' he said. I waved back.

"How's it been, then?" he said.

"Awful."

"Why? What's the matter?"

I sat down and took a sip of my Coke and looked at him.

"I saw you and Lorna today. On the Promenade. At the Fairground. I don't think we should go out together any more." Then he started with the talk, the chat, the words . . . hundreds of them, each one oilier and more untrue than the last . . . all the stuff you've ever heard about . . . Lorna didn't mean anything, just a silly flirtation, it was her fault anyway, she wouldn't leave him alone, won't happen again, you're the one for me . . . round and round the words went in my head, and every so often Grandma Clampitt joined in from round the corner, adding the steel echoes of her voice to Adam's. I listened for ages, but then I decided, all of a sudden, that I'd had enough. I finished the rest of my Coke and stood up.

"I'm going now," I said. "I've learned what

real love is now, so all your stuff won't do any more. The trouble with you is, you think you love me, but you don't. Not really. Not enough. Not enough for me." I turned and started to walk away from the table.

"How much *is* enough for you, then?" he shouted after me. "What the hell do you want? Tell me that ... go on, tell me. I'm waiting to hear."

I called out to him over my shoulder as I stepped into the darkness.

"A longer ride on the Carousel," I shouted and thought that somewhere, far away, I could hear the laughter of the Laughing Clown.

Three Fables

The Female Swan

And then there was the duckling who aspired to be a swan. She worked very hard, studied the history and literature of swans, the growth of their swanhood, their hopes and ideals, and their time-honoured customs. In the end, even the swans acknowledged that this duck had rendered them a signal service. They threw a banquet (no ducks invited) and gave her a paper, which stated clearly that thereafter she would be an Honorary Swan. She was highly gratified, as were some of the ducks, who began to feel that there was hope for them. Others just laughed. "A duck is a duck," they said, "and ought not to aspire to be a swan. A duck, by definition, is inferior to swans." This seemed so evident that they forgot the matter and paddled off. But there were still others who were angered by this. "Those ducks do not think," they said. "But as for the learned one, she has betrayed us to the cause of swans. She is no longer a duck. She is a swan." This too seemed evident. They turned to Andersen. "Well," he said, "there are a great many ducks and a great many duckponds." But that didn't help, so he tried again. "The thing is," he said, "you are beginning to question the nature of ducks and the values of swans." "Yes," they said. "We know," they said, "but where will it end?" "I don't know," said Andersen, "You're learning to fashion your own fables."

THE PROMISE OF KING HILAR

When King Hilar fell off his horse in the middle of the forest and sprained his ankle, he was so grateful to the woman who rescued him that he promised her the thing he treasured most. The woman didn't pay any attention to this. All she saw was that he was hurt and needed help. Whether or not he was King Hilar didn't matter to her. She was happy enough living in the forest and didn't need anything much or promises of things from anyone. And so when the courtiers had been sent for and the king had been rescued and taken care of, she forgot all about him.

But the king didn't forget. He took himself very seriously indeed and felt strongly that a royal promise ought not to be broken. He lay on his couch and thought hard. "Shall I give her my emerald bowl or my golden sword or my silver studded saddle or my beautiful carpet with all the beasts of the forest woven on it in silken threads of a thousand different colours, or shall I give her . . .?" He became confused. He summoned the Royal Treasurer. "Read out a list of all my treasures," the king commanded him.

"Certainly, Your Highness," answered the treasurer, "but it would take weeks and weeks."

A promise was a promise, but the king didn't want to spend weeks on it. He frowned at the treasurer. "Listen," he told him, "just reel off the names of half a dozen treasures I happen to own."

The treasurer said quickly, "Well, Your Majesty, there are the two riding camels, the three elephants – two black and one white – and the Arabian racehorse. There are also – "

"That will do," interrupted the king. "Now send off someone to summon the woman."

"What woman, Your Majesty?" asked the treasurer timidly.

"The woman who rescued me, of course," growled the king. Then he lay back and pretended to sleep because his ankle was hurting him.

The courtiers rode into the forest and brought back the woman who had helped the king. She was a little annoyed at being disturbed in this way, but tried to be nice. The king smiled at her expansively, "Now, dear lady, I have among my possessions two black elephants, one white, two riding camels and a thoroughbred horse. Which of these would you like for yourself?"

"Why, none of them, Your Majesty, though it's kind of you to offer. You see, I live in a small house in the middle of the forest. And where would I put them? And what would they eat?"

"Oh. Well, is there something else you would like instead?"

"Nothing, thank you, Your Majesty," the woman replied.

At this, His Majesty became petulant. "But don't you see, you're getting in the way of a king keeping his solemn promise. Do try to help. Isn't there anything at all that you would really like?"

The woman thought. 'Well," she murmured at last, "I would really like a cup of tea."

"Is that all?" The king was disappointed. "That's too easy."

"But that's what I want," replied the woman. "And you have to make it."

"Oh," said the king. He summoned the Royal Chef. "How," he asked, "do you make a cup of tea?" The Royal Chef explained in detail. "Oh," said the king again. "Well, fetch me some fire and some water and a few tea leaves." Then the king limped about and finally produced a weak cup of tea. He handed it to the woman who had waited patiently through all this fuss. "Thank you," she said. She drank it politely, and then she returned to the forest where she lived happily.

WOLF

There was once a young woman who made friends with a wolf. At first the men were filled with admiration. "It's because she's a virgin," they would whisper slyly. "Look, how even the wild beasts fear her. She has tamed the wolves." All this was nonsense, of course. There had never been any question of taming. It was simply that the woman and the wolf got on, and frequently went for walks together. But as time went by and the virgin continued to remain a virgin, and the wolf continued to remain a wolf, the men became peevish. "The fact is," they explained to one another, "she uses the wolf to guard her virginity. The man who would win her must slay the wolf." The story spread, the hunters got ready and a great wolf-hunting expedition was organized. The virgin was asked to serve as bait. "That isn't good sense," the virgin protested; but the hunters said that they were in charge and understood these matters. In the end they tied the virgin to a tree in the forest and hid among the bushes. They waited for the wolf. No sign of a wolf. By the following morning they were tired and hungry so they returned to their houses and slept all day. At night they were back. Still no wolf and no

84

virgin either. A sure sign, they told one another, of the presence of wolves. All night long they ranged through the forest. They grew tired. They fell asleep in the forest. They woke up and hunted and fell asleep again. They were thoroughly lost, but night after night they hunted for virgins and also for wolves. In the end the elders decided that the forest had swallowed the hunters, so they put a sign on the edge of their town in large red letters warning the unwary that there were wolves about.

Subsequent History

The subsequent history of the young woman and that of the wolf is harder to trace. Once they had eluded the hunters they looked at one another ruefully. "Perhaps in some other country, some other forest . . .," murmured the wolf. They were very tired and wanted to rest. But the first set of villagers they came upon hemmed and hawed and finally said well, all right, they could stay provided the wolf was thoroughly examined and had every tooth and claw removed. When they approached the next village the wolf tried to look as harmless as possible, but this lot weren't interested in the wolf. They told the young woman that it was necessary for her to marry one of them and settle down at once. And so the two friends walked away, and when at the third village they were rudely greeted by sticks and stones, because, it was claimed, their reputation had preceded them, they were not greatly surprised, but just walked on until at last they entered a realm that is not, as yet, familiar to us.

Bargain Basement

"Shall we go somewhere else?" she said, speaking first and why not. She had finished her plate of eggs, chips and beans and so had he and the noise of the transport cafe, juke-box and the rattle of crocks, was deafening. She had sat at his table because she liked the look of him — thick black hair like a horse's tail, a swarthy skin, bit of Indian blood could be, and fantastic eyes, clear green like wine bottles. She liked his ragged jerkin and his headband too, for different reasons. They had been exchanging covert or less covert glances since she sat down.

"Don't mind," he said, grinning and showing a bonus of even white teeth. "Hang about."

He got up and crossed to the fruit machine, waiting his turn. He was quite tall, she saw now, and his jeans were tattered almost to the point of indecency. Beautiful, she thought dreamily, as he dropped in 10p and pulled the knob. There was a pinging sound and then a clatter that crescendoed and went on and on as a mound of coins filled the tray and spilled out all over the floor. He kneeled down, sweeping them together with both hands and dropping them into his ancient striped haversack.

"Know something?" he said, pushing the cafe door with a slight swagger. "You're lucky, see, you and me."

"You think so," she said, pouting doubtfully. *Lucky* was what they all said, her parents, Annabel at school, Mrs Green who "did" for her mother four days a week. "Born with a silver spoon in your mouth, you were," Mrs Green said.

But she didn't feel lucky. She felt stifled. Trapped. Parents with loads of money and loads of talent, parents who really liked each other and the Persian carpets and antique furniture with which they had filled the house, such advantage wasn't necessarily lucky. Not if you weren't talented or clever and had "A" levels coming up next week. Sometimes she had to get out. Get away. Escape. It was why she had taken off on Friday night, hitched right up the M1 and on again towards Carlisle. She had done it before, gone off without a word, not knowing where. A statement. It worried them to death, of course.

"What do you want to do then?" he said as they crossed the lorry park. There was a lilt to his voice. "Where do you want to go?"

"Up there," she said, pointing. It was late May and away from the main road and the stream of traffic was a great expanse of hillside, moor, craggy and dotted with gorse, outlined against blue sky. He went first, moving quickly, leaning forward with his haversack bouncing on his slim back. Like those mountain goats near the entrance to Regents Park Zoo, she thought, struggling to keep up and soon out of breath.

"Hey, wait," she cried out. "Wait." He turned at her plaintive wail and stood looking down. She was nothing special to look at, friendly bunround face and hair dyed scarlet on top like a tousled chrysanthemum but he liked her eyes, the way she looked at him, so hopeful, so eager. He needed girls to look at him like that.

"You're too fat," he said.

"I know," she said humbly.

"Come on then," he said and took her hand. He climbed more slowly after that, pulling her after him but glancing back now and then and smiling. About halfway up she collapsed, choosing, he noticed, a grassy hollow well-screened with gorse and a stunted hawthorn to fling herself down.

"I'm puffed out," she said. "And I think you're beautiful."

"Beautiful?" he said, standing on a rock just above the hollow, considering her compliment, her gift. A skylark trilled in the sky above.

"Do you want to?" she said. He murmured something vague, looking away across the hills. Eager girls were all very well. "Have you got one?" she said. "You needn't worry about me. I've been on the pill for yonks." But it wasn't *her* he was worried about.

"Well, anyway, I still think you're beautiful," she said generously. She was a generous girl and not even miffed. She sat up and pushed her shirt down into her jeans. "Where do you come from then?"

"The valleys," he said, turning to gaze in what he estimated was a southerly direction. "South Wales. My dad's down the pits, been down since he was fifteen."

"But not you?" she said wonderingly. It seemed such a terrible life, dreadful, but wonderful too, so elemental, so real.

"No way," he said. "Like the sky above my head, don't I? Be like a prison to me, see, stuck down the pits. The only life there is for a man, according to my dad."

"So you just took off?" she said. She had never met anybody else who did it. "Escaped?"

"You could say," he said, aware of a new light in her eyes.

"Where you been then?" Her gaze fixed on him. Taking off was real, life on the road was real. "Travelling all the time, bet you been some places?"

"All over," he said cautiously. What did her lit-up eyes precisely need to fuel them? "Night here, few days there. Spent some time with the Hippy Convoy."

"The Rainbow People?"

"That's right. Saw the police in Savernake Forest smash the vans right up . . . windscreens . . . slashed tyres . . ."

"Saw that on the telly," she said. "Pigs."

"Do you mind?" he said, thrusting his nose against her and making snuffling, grunting noises. "Some of my best friends are pigs."

"You're really something," she said, laughing and loving him already, her eyes glowing like stars.

"You're not bad yourself," he said, kissing her gently.

They stayed there all night, leaving the grassy hollow and moving down towards the woods as the sun slid towards the horizon. He was surprisingly resourceful, had a Stanley knife in his haversack and a tiny cooking stove with tablets of solid fuel and a plastic sheet. He cut long branches and made a bender tent, foraged along the edge of a field and came back with potatoes, two eggs, nettles, comfrey, and made a stew which was at least edible. She had never been so happy, so in tune with the moment. In all her takings off she had never found anyone like this. She knew now that all this time she had been not just running away but searching. And she had found what she was searching for. A travelling man. They slept side by side to keep warm, and, snuggled tight against his back in the early dawn, she had decided.

"Would you like to come home with me?"

"What?" he said.

"Back to my place. I mean you could stay as long as you like. But the thing is," she added casually, "I've got these crappy exams next week."

"Are you sure?" he said. "I mean . . . your parents . . ."

"Oh, they don't care about anything as long as I take my 'A' levels." She glanced at him anxiously. She hadn't said 'A' levels before in case it put him off.

"Still . . . they might not want me stopping?" He didn't know about Oxford and wanting her to have all they had had and all that shit. She couldn't see the point herself. "Where do you live anyway?"

"London," she said. "Islington. I mean we got this big house practically empty with only the three of us. It's wicked really, I'm always telling them."

"And you're sure your parents won't mind?" He did rather fancy London. He'd only been the once when he was small. The Tower and a pantomine, Puss in Boots.

"Course not," she grinned mischievously. "They'll be worried out of their minds by this time. Won't care about a thing just as long as I'm back. Honestly." She said it quite blithely. Her parents said she mustn't feel guilty and she tried not to but she always did.

On Sunday evening they walked along the road where she lived, a Georgian terrace like a tall cliff. It was almost dark. She had phoned from Heston Service Station just an hour before.

"This is us," she said. There was a little paved courtyard with plants in tubs and steps leading up to the front door.

"Oh, Daisy, darling, you awful, awful girl," her mother said, running out, tall and willowy, a portrait painter, enfolding her daughter in her arms. "Why do you do it? Why?"

"Sorry, Mummy," Daisy said over and over. "Sorry."

"Well, she's back now anyway." Her father was brighter, older, editor of a literary magazine, a short man with a neat beard and a black velvet jacket. "I don't think you mentioned your friend's name?"

"Ben," said Ben, offering his hand. "Pleased to meet you."

Her father shook it warmly. "Pleased to meet you too, Ben. Your mother's been worried sick, young lady," he added. "I suppose you realize that? And your exams next week."

"Well, I'm back now, aren't I?" Daisy said

sulkily. "Anyway they don't start until Thursday. And I'm absolutely famished."

"There's turkey sandwiches," her mother said gaily. "I just this minute made them. And the spare room's all ready for your friend."

"He's sleeping in my room," Daisy said. "And we don't need anybody rapping on about condoms either. All right?"

Silence. A long pause.

"But ... but it's school tomorrow, don't forget."

"I know," said Daisy.

"I'll be quite okay in the spare room," Ben said.

"Thank you for bringing her home, young man," her father said.

"He didn't," Daisy said, taking a third turkey sandwich and steering Ben firmly towards her bedroom. "I brought him."

He felt badly then, eating their sandwiches and upsetting them. After all it wasn't his home and she wasn't his girl and he wasn't all that sure he wanted her to be, too posh and too shameless. He had been moved out on the hill, startled by her incompetence and flattered by her admiration of his skills. Well, he hadn't been in the Scouts all those years for nothing. But now she was behaving like a spoilt child, asking for a slap, Mam would have said.

He had never seen anything like her bedroom

though. Every bit of wall covered with posters, Zooga, Bob Marley, James Dean, Jimi Hendrix, UB 40 glowering or smiling all round made him feel quite nervous taking off his clothes.

"I think you're beautiful," she whispered and her brown spaniel eyes had such wanting, such pleading, it really got to him. "So beautiful and so gorgeous," she whispered on and on into the darkness. All girls were a bit different, he supposed, but he'd never met one as enthusiastic as this. Never.

In the morning she looked wan, almost bedraggled when she put on her school skirt and blazer. They had cornflakes in the kitchen in silence, nobody else seemed to be up, and then he walked her to school carrying her satchel.

"Promise me you won't run away," she said at the school gates, giving him her key. "I couldn't bear it if you did, I'd simply die." She seemed to mean it. "Promise me you'll stay. Don't let them get at you."

"I promise," he said. No girl had ever looked at him as she did. He needed the way she looked at him. But he only had the week. He wandered in an adjacent park for a bit and then went back to the house and let himself in.

"Is that you, Ben? Would you come in here a minute?" her mother called from the studio. This is it, he thought, chucking out time. Her smock was daubed with paint, she wiped her hands on a rag nervously. There were dark rings under her eyes as if she hadn't slept. "I think we ought to talk." She paused but Ben said nothing so she went on. "Daisy's got her exams at the end of the week. She must give proper time to her revision and she must get a full night's sleep if she's to get decent grades. Well it's important . . . er . . . you do understand?"

"Yes," said Ben.

"My husband and I . . . Oh, dear, that sounds like the Queen on Christmas day, doesn't it?"

"You want me to go?" said Ben. "The thing is, I promised Daisy, see . . ."

"No. Oh, no. Goodness me . . . we don't want to spoil anything." She put her hand on his arm, quite stricken. "We think everybody should do what they want as long as it doesn't . . . er . . . interfere with anybody else. Of course you must stay, Ben. It's just we thought you might like to have the basement. It's quite self-contained, we used to let it at one time. We thought if you had the basement, you might like to do it up? I mean we'd pay you of course. Then . . . well . . . it'd give you something to do while Daisy gets on with her studying. The thing is . . . I thought . . . we thought . . . if you were to put the idea to her . . ."

"Sort of a deal like?" he said. "A bargain?"

"If you like," she said with a little laugh. "Er

. . . what do you think, I mean a bargain has to suit everybody doesn't it?"

"I think . . ." his green eyes considered her warily and circled. There was a portrait on the easel, a face vaguely familiar. He wondered if she was famous as a painter. "I think we'd better have a look at the basement."

"It's rather dusty, I'm afraid," she said as he followed her down the stairs. There were two large square rooms with windows level to the ground outside and covered with a grille. In the front they looked onto the courtyard and the pavement, at the back onto a lawn and a vista of trees. There was some scrappy furniture, throw-outs from the house and items too large to move, a mattress on the floor, a small bathroom and a kitchen across the narrow hall. Done up you could get two hundred a week for a flat like this, he reckoned, and here she was offering it to him free, or more or less. He'd always had a winning streak, his stars according to Mam. He tested the taps in the bathroom and pulled the plug with what he hoped was a shrewd expression.

"Gas stove work?" he said.

"Of course, and there's an electric kettle some-where," she said. "And constant hot water. The central heating goes on with ours. I mean it's the same system . . ." Did she think he was going to stay that long?

"How much?" he said. "I mean if I was to do the place up for you?"

"Does a hundred pounds seem all right?" she said. "I mean we'll be paying for the paint of course . . . and bed and board."

"Sounds fair," he said quietly. "But I'll have to talk it over with Daisy."

"Oh, I quite see that."

Daisy liked the idea. Her eyes were no less loving when he met her out of school but they were puffy with scribbling revision notes all day.

"A place of our own," she said slowly. "Doesn't seem a lot wrong with that? If we can paint it any way we want?"

"If *I* can," said Ben sternly. That was the bargain and he wasn't into ripping people off. "You've got to be doing three hours' homework every evening and getting a good night's sleep."

"Okay, okay," she said, gazing at him lovingly. She didn't mind anything as long as he stayed. A travelling man with eyes as green as go signs. "As long as it lasts."

"You're beautiful," she whispered that night, over and over. He had never known a girl who liked it so much. "So beautiful . . . gorgeous."

She let Ben choose the colours. She didn't care about anything as long as he stayed. He painted every wall in the front room different, black, blue, green, brown. Black was for coal, she said, blue was sky, green was the grass on top and brown was pit ponies. He didn't have the heart to tell her that there hadn't been pit ponies in his village for forty years. He painted steadily all day and through the evening while Daisy got on with her homework, now and then making forays to the fridge upstairs for food for them both. Food was part of the bargain and he didn't fancy facing her parents over the table for meals. He kept out of their way and that of the cleaning woman as much as possible. He did get a bit sick of cold food.

The only innovation was that Daisy insisted on sleeping on the mattress downstairs despite the dirt and smell of paint. In fact the squalor seemed to excite her. Ben grumbled a bit but then found he liked it better too. The bedroom walls weren't all that thick and this way he wasn't always meeting her dad on the way to the toilet.

Thursday Daisy did her first English Literature paper and Ben painted the bathroom yellow. Friday she had French and he painted the kitchen red.

"Yellow as margarine and red as tomato ketchup is beautiful," Daisy said, whirling exultantly. Two tough days had come and gone. "And you're beautiful too." Girls had said it before but nobody had ever said it quite like Daisy.

"I got to go," he muttered that night.

"You can't," said Daisy. "Oh stay, please stay . . . do you want me to fail? . . . do you want me to ruin my whole life? Stay, oh stay . . . say you don't have to go?"

He did have to go. It was the end of his fortnight's holiday and he was due back at Merthyr the following Monday. But he didn't like to tell her that and see the light die in her eyes. He couldn't. The way she looked at him had him bewitched. It was like an addiction. She had made him into a different person.

"Better stay then," he muttered and she covered him with kisses.

The second week he painted the back room walls, orange, violet, grey, white and Daisy did both History papers and her second French. They both finished at the same time.

"Can we come down?" her father called from the top of the basement stairs.

"If you like . . ." said Daisy.

"Terrific," they said, wandering from room to room, blinking at the vivid colours. "Congratulations to you both. I think this calls for a celebration. Champagne? And we thought we'd get a take-away. Indian or Chinese, Daisy darling?"

"Ben can choose," Daisy said. "And don't forget you owe him."

"Of course, of course," her father said. "A hundred pounds wasn't it?"

"Exploitation. You'd have to pay a decorator twice as much," Daisy grumbled.

"Help yourselves, everybody," Daisy's mother said, unloading silver boxes of chicken vindaloo, chicken tandoori, prawn curry and lamb kebabs across the kitchen table. "Help yourself, Ben."

"Thanks," said Ben.

"Try the vindaloo, it's really good," her father said, entering into the spirit and spooning it onto their plates. He lifted his glass. "Here's to Daisy and a bright future."

"Knickers," said Daisy. "Must you, Daddy?"

"Daisy," said Ben, raising his glass.

"Ben," said Daisy, raising hers.

"And what about you, young man? Any plans?"

"He's staying here," Daisy said.

"He's certainly entitled to a few days' rest, you both are," her father said. "But after that . . . well there are various possibilities."

"Such as?" Daisy said suspiciously.

"YTS schemes, Tops courses, all sorts of things . . . That flat looks quite . . . er, professional. Had any kind of job, have you, Ben? Any useful work experience?"

"We're not all enslaved to the work ethic like you, Daddy," Daisy said. "Some people think there's more to life than working their guts out nine to five and paying the rotten mortgage." She smiled at Ben encouragingly. "Besides, he's got gypsy blood."

"Is that right?" her mother said. "How fascinating, Ben."

'My grandma was a gypsy," Ben said, embarrassed. "Grew up on the road."

"There you are then," said Daisy, chewing curried prawns. "It explains everything. Why, you're a travelling man."

"But I never knew her," Ben said. "She died young, it was living in a house killed her, see?"

"Sad," Daisy's mother said. "Poor woman. I expect she missed the excitement . . . things changing . . ."

"Still, there are these YTS schemes," her father persisted. "Cater for all sorts and conditions . . . I mean you don't have to have any qualifications at all . . ."

"Matter of fact I . . ." Ben said, nettled.

"It's always the same bloody thing," Daisy interrupted. "Bring anybody home and Daddy starts interfering . . . poking his nose. Why don't you ask him about his prospects? Wouldn't put it past you."

"Did you get a CSE at all?" her father said, ignoring her. "Every little helps, you know."

"You think . . ." Ben was suddenly furious, wagging his finger. "You think I'm some sort of layabout, don't you? I've got five fucking 'O' levels, thanks very much, and a job as a matter of fact, had it ever since I left school, clerk with the Coal Board. Least I did have," he added. He didn't want to go back, certainly not, this thing with Daisy had changed everything but he couldn't help wondering whether they'd have him back.

"Coal Board?" said Daisy. Her eyes had turned opaque and dull as puddles, suddenly they filled with tears. "Coal Board?"

"What's the matter?" Ben said that night. "What have I done?"

"Nothing." She turned away. "Nothing at all." She didn't understand it either. Why had "Clerk at the Coal Board" turned her body lifeless like ancient wood? She gazed at the grille on the windows. "This place is like a prison . I'm sick of people telling me what to do."

"Nobody's telling you what to do," he said, saddened and reduced. She was never going to say he was beautiful again and there was nothing he could do.

Two days later Daisy took off. Her parents were worried of course but not as worried as they had been. She had done her "A" levels after all. She would land on her feet, she always did. Ben stayed one more night and took off with a hundred pounds in his pocket. He felt better moving, alive again, hitching down the M4 towards the South West, almost as if he could feel Daisy's adoring gaze warming him again. She didn't have his address or even know his name.

He was glad about that, couldn't have her turning up out of the blue, Mam would have a fit.

He didn't go home in the end. Somehow he had to keep travelling. Taking off he felt so great, felt just as he had when Daisy looked at him that special way.

Season followed season but time did not have much meaning on the road. Travelling. One day as he wandered along the pavement cradling a package of chips he suddenly stopped, spreading the greasy paper on the top of a garden wall. A photograph of a white wedding at Oxford.

"Posh," he murmured. "Aw, shit."

How long ago was it? The newspaper was a fortnight old. A travelling man. Had he got the obsession from Daisy or was it, as people sometimes said, just the gypsy wanderlust coming out?

Ben glanced down at her wedding photograph again and then crumpled the newspaper into a ball. It was time to get back on the road.

THE CONTRIBUTORS

ROSEMARY STONES (compiler)
Rosemary Stones has written studies of gender presentation in children's literature (*Pour Out the Cocoa, Janet* etc) and non-fiction books for teenagers on sex education and on sexual violence. She compiled *More to Life Than Mr Right: Stories for Young Feminists* (Piccadilly/Tracks).

JACQUELINE ROY
A Family Likeness is based on Jacqueline Roy's own family history – her father was the celebrated Jamaican sculptor, Namba Roy. Jacqueline's first novel, *Soul Daddy*, is published by Collins.

SANDRA CHICK
Sandra Chick's powerful first novel, *Push Me, Pull Me* (Livewires) dealing with sexual abuse in the family, won the 1987 Other Award. Sandra lives in Bath.

SUSANNAH BOWYER
Susannah Bowyer lived at Greenham Peace Camp for 18 months. In 1988 she abseiled into the House of Lords to protest against Clause 28 of the Local Government bill. *On the Verge* is her first published story.

Adèle Geras

Adèle Geras lives in Manchester. Her feminism comes across in the range of female characters she includes in her work and in the themes she tackles, for example, in *The Green Behind the Glass* and *Voyage* (Hamish Hamilton/Tracks).

Suniti Namjoshi

Suniti Namjoshi's latest collection of feminist fables is *The Blue Donkey Fables* (Women's Press). *Wolf* and *The Promise of King Hilar* are published by kind permission of Gay Sweatshop who commissioned them for their 1989 women's project. Born in India, Suniti now lives in Devon.

Geraldine Kaye

Geraldine Kaye has written many novels for children and young people, often addressing the theme of cultural differences. Her novel, *Comfort Herself* (Deutsch/Magnet) won the 1985 Other Award. Geraldine lives in Bristol.

LIONS · TRACKS

That Was Then, This Is Now

S. E. Hinton

Bryon and Mark had always been like brothers but at sixteen they began to drift apart. After establishing his popularity with the girls, Bryon fell seriously in love with Cathy, while Mark spent more time hustling and making lots of money from his secret activities. But they were still inseparable.

Then Charlie, the barman, got killed defending Bryon and Mark in an ugly brawl. Mark called it fate. 'Things happen, that's all there is to it.' But it bothered Bryon, and for the first time he realized, 'I was changing and he wasn't.'

The split between the boys continues to grow, when Bryon gets a job after school and tries to help save Cathy's younger brother M & M from hard drugs. And then one day Bryon discovers the awful truth about Mark . . .

'A starkling realistic book, a punch from the shoulder which leaves the reader considerably shaken.'
Times Literary Supplement

LIONS · TRACKS

A Question of Courage

Marjorie Darke

Em could hardly credit her own daring – here she was, Emily Palmer from the back streets of Birmingham, carrying a placard that boldly read VOTES FOR WOMEN in a bicycle parade, and on a Sunday too! But Em had been swept into the cause by the eloquent Louise Marshall, and though their lives were worlds apart, Emily knew she'd had enough of being a 'bloomin' slave'. Already she'd spent five years sewing for a pittance and she was only eighteen.

The night that Emily and Louise were caught red-handed painting slogans on the golf course sealed both their friendship and their fight. Then came London and Mrs Pankhurst's Suffragette Movement, and the cloak and dagger fun was over. Now it was rallies, imprisonment, and most terrible of all, force feeding. But as the movement and its violence grew, so did Emily's self-doubts, and for her the choice of continuing the fight became a question of courage.

Confessions of a Teenage Baboon

Paul Zindel

Lloyd sprang like an animal, grabbed Chris by the shoulders, and slammed him up against the door. "I'm not finished with you," he said, "because there's a few things I've been wanting to tell you, and one of them is that you're retarded. I mean you're out of it. You don't know anything about being a man . . . if you had a father you might not be such a loser."

No one had ever talked to Chris like this; besides, it wasn't really his fault that he was a loser. His father had cleared off years ago and left him alone with his mother, Helen, who was not only loud and domineering, but a kleptomaniac to boot. All that Chris had to remind him of his father was a mangy old coat which he hoped he'd be big enough to wear one day.

The summer that Chris is fifteen, he and Helen move to the Dipardi house where Helen is hired as a nurse for Lloyd Dipardi's dying mother. Lloyd, a thirty-year-old drunken shipyard worker, who keeps the house full of misfit teenagers and gives wild parties, takes an instant dislike to Chris, taunting him for his scruffiness and giving him a hard time. But it is Lloyd who shocks Chris into standing up for himself and taking responsibility for his own life, who makes Chris realize that "Kid, it's up to you. You don't have to be a loser."

"Paul Zindel handles the stuff of teenage life with a delicacy at once funny and heartfelt, outspoken and sensitive." *TLS*